This book belongs to:

....

....

For Blake, my inspirational little dragon
and Leo, for saving our little bird – SQ

For my little dragon Eddie – AJ

Quarto is the authority on a wide range of topics.

Quarto educates, entertains and enriches the lives of
our readers—enthusiasts and lovers of hands-on living.

www.quartoknows.com

Designer: Victoria Kimonidou
Editor: Matthew Morgan

Copyright © QED Publishing 2016
First published in the UK in 2016 by QED Publishing

Part of The Quarto Group
The Old Brewery
6 Blundell Street
London N7 9BH

A catalogue record for this book is available from
the British Library.

ISBN 978 1 78493 785 0

Printed in China

THE littlest DRAGON

Susan Quinn

Illustrated by Ag Jatkowska

Long ago, when dragons roamed Earth,
Mrs Dragon sat waiting for her eggs to hatch.

She smiled as the first egg went CRACK!

She smiled as the second egg went CRACK!

But when the third egg went CRACK...

Mrs Dragon gasped.
Out popped the littlest dragon
she had ever seen.

"Mama!"
said the
Littlest Dragon.

"Aren't you sweet?"
Mrs Dragon said.

"Dragons aren't sweet!" snorted Mr Dragon. "They're big and strong!"

But the Littlest Dragon didn't grow big and strong.

His legs were too short to run fast.

He was last in the flying races because his wings were too small.

Even worse, he could not breathe fire, however hard he tried.

"Whoever heard of a dragon who can't breathe fire?" laughed the other dragons.

Each day the Littlest Dragon grew more sad and lonely. "I'm such a rubbish dragon," he sobbed.

Little Bird fluttered down from her tree.

"I will help you find a way to **breathe fire**," she said.

"How can you help?" sniffed the Littlest Dragon. "You're not a dragon!"

"I can be your friend," Little Bird replied.

'Then winter came.

Mr and Mrs Dragon had colds.

The Littlest Dragon's brothers had colds.

And when dragons have colds, they can't breathe fire.
And without their fire, dragons can't keep warm.

"I will find someone to light our fire," said the Littlest Dragon.

And off he went.

The Littlest Dragon ran to every house in the valley.

But every dragon in the valley had a cold, and every fire had gone out.

All the dragons were freezing.

"Please help us!" they croaked.

"If only I could breathe fire!" cried the Littlest Dragon.

Suddenly, Little
Bird had an idea.

She plucked a feather from her wing and
tickled the end of the Littlest Dragon's nose.

The Littlest Dragon's nose began to itch...

The Littlest Dragon's nose began to twitch...

It itched and twitched!

And then...

Two fireballs shot out of his nostrils.

"I BREATHED FIRE!"
yelled the Littlest Dragon.

Soon, every dragon in the valley
had a fire to keep them warm.

"You're a hero,"
Mr Dragon said proudly.

"I could never have done it without Little Bird," the Littlest Dragon replied.

He looked at the feather and smiled.

He might never win running or flying races but he could breathe fire. And with Little Bird as his friend, he would never be lonely again.

Next Steps

After reading the story, look at the front cover again. Could the children have guessed what the story was about just by looking at the front cover?

The other dragons made fun of the Littlest Dragon because he couldn't breathe fire. Ask the children if they have made fun of someone who couldn't do something or if someone has made fun of them.

When reading the story, did the children think that Little Bird would be able to help the Littlest Dragon?

Ask the children to discuss how it feels to finally do something they have been trying to do for a long time.

In the story, Little Bird is the Littlest Dragon's best friend. Ask the children who is their best friend, and why.

Discuss with the children how it often helps to do things together as a team. Can they think of a time they achieved something with the help of their friends?

Why is fire so important to the dragons in the story? Discuss with the children how fire can be dangerous too.

Ask the children if they think dragons are real, and why. Ask them to create their own dragon. They could make a collage, cutting out shiny paper scales and sticking on red and yellow tissue paper for fire.

Show the children the Welsh flag (don't tell them where it comes from) and draw their attention to the red dragon on it. Ask them if they can they name the country whose flag it is.